BACK
THAT
THING

STEPHANIE PERRY MOORE

THE *SWOOP* LIST #3

BACK THAT THING

STEPHANIE PERRY MOORE

MINNEAPOLIS

Darby Creek
A division of Lerner Publishing Group, Inc.
241 First Avenue North
Minneapolis, MN 55401 USA

For reading levels and more information, look up this title at
www.lernerbooks.com.

Cover: © iStockphoto.com/kate_sept2004 (teen girl); © Andrew Marginean/
Dreamstime.com (brick hall background); © Andrew Scherbackov/
Shutterstock.com (notebook paper).

Interior: © Andrew Marginean/Dreamstime.com (brick hall background);
© Sam74100/Dreamstime.com, pp. 1, 38, 69; © Luba V Nel/Dreamstime.
com, pp. 9, 45, 76; © iStockphoto.com/kate_sept2004, pp. 16, 51, 82;
© Hemera Technologies/AbleStock.com/Thinkstock, pp. 24, 57, 88;
© Rauluminate/iStock/Thinkstock, pp. 31, 63, 95.

Main body text set in Janson Text LT Std 12/17.5.
Typeface provided by Adobe Systems.

Library of Congress Cataloging-in-Publication Data

Moore, Stephanie Perry.
    Back that thing / by Stephanie Perry Moore.
        pages   cm. — (The Swoop List ; #3)
    Summary: The "Swoop List" girls are forced to examine their pasts and
why their names are on that roster of so-called sluts, as well as what they
should do—individually and in support of one another—to turn things
around.
    ISBN 978-1-4677-5806-2 (lib. bdg. : alk. paper)
    ISBN 978-1-4677-6051-5 (pbk.)
    ISBN 978-1-4677-6193-2 (eBook pdf)
    [1. Conduct of life—Fiction. 2. Dating (Social customs)—Fiction.
3. Sex—Fiction. 4. Interpersonal relations—Fiction. 5. High schools—
Fiction. 6. Schools—Fiction.] I. Title.
PZ7.M788125Bac 2015
[Fic]—dc23   2014027381

Manufactured in the United States of America
1 – SB – 12/31/14

For
my debutantes

Autumn Astin
Kaylyn Becton
Angel Carter
Gloria Clark
Devin Edwards
Taylor Evans
Candace Kenney
Taylor Jackson
Keyarria Mack
Sydni Moore
My'esha Robinson
Darby Thorne

You are budding roses,
blooming and blossoming.
Continue to look in the mirror and
love the beautiful creation reflected there!

CHAPTER ONE

Hater (Sanaa's Beginning)

As Sanaa Mathis pulled up to the group home after Olive Bell called her in hysterics, asking her to come over because they desperately needed to talk, Sanaa reflected on all that was going on with her new group of friends, the swoop list girls. These girls had been ostracized by their community after they were put on a list of so-called easy girls, the swoop list. But they'd now come together to help each other. They changed the meaning of the swoop list by swooping into each other's lives and encouraging each other to take control of their situations.

However, when Sanaa took a walk down

memory lane in her own life, as close as she was to her new friends, she did miss her old friend Toni. Sanaa and Toni had been friends since nursery school. Over the years, Sanaa had gotten used to their healthy competition. Every time Sanaa did something, Toni wanted to do it too. It was like they had the same taste in everything: dresses, extracurricular activities, and—as they got to high school—boys. One boy in particular, Miles, had both of their eyes. Miles had arrived at Jackson High School as a junior, and every girl in the school wanted him. Toni was too shy to go after him, so she asked Sanaa to approach him. Sanaa did, but instead of Miles wanting Toni, he wanted Sanaa. Sanaa could never break it to her friend that she'd liked him all along too. Deep down, she felt like a traitor.

So with this new group of girls, Sanaa didn't want to mess things up. She didn't want to compete with them or compare herself to them. She wanted to be happy for them when they had stuff that she didn't have. But as Sanaa parked in front of the group home to see Olive, she was reminded again that Olive didn't even have parents. Sanaa felt privileged. Though her family struggled to pay the bills and she barely ever had new stuff, at least she had a family.

As soon as Olive opened up the door, Sanaa hugged her tight. Olive smiled and said, "What? I know I sounded desperate on the phone, but I'm okay."

"No, I know. I just wanted to tell you I appreciate you."

"Well, thank you for coming over here! Girl, you gotta see this. This is crazy, and I'm just stressed because Charles has got to go in front of a judge tomorrow." Charles had been Olive's foster brother, but recently they'd discovered they had deep romantic feelings for each other. But after some fights with gang members, Charles was in trouble with the law.

"Can I help?" Sanaa asked.

"I wish someone could. I don't know how this will turn out, but they're talking about removing Charles from the group home."

Clutching her heart, Sanaa said, "Are you serious?"

Trying not to cry, Olive said, "Yes."

As Sanaa thought about it, maybe it wasn't so bad. Maybe removing Charles would eliminate all the gang tension. Because Charles wasn't trying to let up on revenge against the Black Oil gang that had shot up the group home and injured his foster brother, Shawn, Sanaa believed things were only going to get more violent.

Sanaa knew her girlfriend needed her support, so she kept her opinion to herself and changed the subject. "You just said you got some weird message, right?"

Olive grabbed her bag and reached inside. "Yeah, earlier I go into my book bag to pull out my book, and I find this."

Shaking, Sanaa said, "Oh my gosh."

"I think it's from that girl, Leah, who keeps writing to us."

"But she's dead. How is she writing this if she's dead?" Sanaa started shaking harder when she took the paper from Olive to check it out.

It read:

Dear Swoop List Girl,

I'm applauding you from heaven, can't you hear? Y'all have come together. Y'all are believing, but now you need to look within and undo your wrongs. Let's call a spade a spade. You're on the swoop list for a reason. You and your friends need to examine what that reason is and take care of it.

Leah

"I'm getting a little tired of this guessing game. If she's dead, she can't really be the one writing these notes," Olive said in an irritated voice.

"I know. But who is sending us these letters, then? Who is she, and why does she care about us?"

"I don't know, but we need to find out."

Sanaa nodded. "Yeah, we need to find out."

The two girls hugged. Sanaa encouraged Olive to hold on. But she believed deep down everything was going to be okay with Charles. That was all Olive needed to hear to reciprocate with another big hug before Sanaa got in her car.

But Sanaa just didn't want to drive home. She knew that what she'd been putting off for a long time needed to be dealt with now. So, consciously, she drove over to Toni's house.

When she saw Toni's car in the driveway, she texted her and said, "Hey. R U there? Im in ur driveway. I wanna talk."

She waited seven minutes, and finally Toni texted back, "I guess U can come in."

"Are you coming in or what?" Toni said in a nasty way when she opened the door. "I can't believe you'd just show up to my house. I could've been entertaining company, but I guess you think the boys just want you and your friends."

"No. I didn't say that at all." Sanaa stepped into the entryway. "But it sounds like you're saying that my friends and I are the only ones that could be entertaining a boy. Contrary to what that stupid list says, we didn't deserve to be on it. No one does."

"But you *are* on the list," Toni said as she looked at Sanaa like she was trash. "So now what? What did you want to say to me? Why are you here?"

Instead of being prideful and turning around to walk away because she knew she already had the one thing Toni wanted, Sanaa breathed deeply and said, "Our relationship has gotten off track, and I'm gonna take full responsibility for that. I've been keeping something from you, and—"

"And what?"

"Remember when you asked me to talk to Miles for you?"

"Yeah. You came back and basically said he didn't give you an answer about me. You told me everything. What else is there to say?" Toni said, looking suspicious.

"I guess what I didn't share is that Miles said he liked *me*."

Toni rolled her eyes and yelled, "You mean you gave him things he wanted, so he liked you! You pleased him, so he had no choice but to like you. You trumped me with your body, and he chose you. You never had the gall to tell me. Is that what you're telling me?"

"No, it wasn't like that."

"What was it like, Sanaa?"

"I liked him too. But I wasn't trying to throw myself on him when I went to him. I told him about you, but he started saying all these things about me, and I just—"

"What? You couldn't be a real best friend? You're nothing but a tramp. Get out my house!" Toni said as she pushed Sanaa toward the door.

Toni pushed so hard that Sanaa's head hit the door with a bang. When Sanaa saw Toni charging toward her, she kicked her in the stomach. The two of them started wrestling.

"I'm so glad we ain't friends no more. You're such a traitor!" Toni said as she yanked some of Sanaa's hair.

"Stop! You're gonna pull my hair out!"

But Toni wouldn't stop, so Sanaa yanked on Toni's hair and said, "What? I'm gonna pull your weave out. This is why I didn't tell you, because it's always about you! Who cares what Miles and I were feeling. Anything I got, you always want. You were never my best friend. You're just my best hater."

CHAPTER TWO

Spoiler (Willow's Beginning)

Willow Dean was sprawled out across her bed, looking up at the ceiling as she talked on the phone with Pia Alvarez, one of the other swoop list girls. A couple of weeks ago, Pia ran away from home because her mother's boyfriend had crossed boundaries and come on to her. With Willow's mom being a pastor and all, Pia felt safe staying there, and she did for a week. But then Pia went back home. Willow hadn't seen her around school and wanted to make sure that she was okay.

"You didn't have to leave here, you know?" Willow told Pia.

"Yeah, but things were getting a little tight around your house too, and I just didn't wanna overstay my welcome."

Willow rolled over and buried her head in her pillow and started kicking her feet. Willow knew Pia was right. Things at her house were far from normal. Her parents had been arguing, practically nonstop. If it wasn't about dinner, it was about finances. But the biggest blowup of all happened around Willow's confessions.

Back in January, when Willow's parents got onto her about their disappointment surrounding her promiscuous behavior, she shut both of them down, claiming they had no right to judge her. Her mom cringed when she talked about her dad's porno stash, and her dad was furious when she talked about the sex toys her mom had. At the time, Willow didn't realize that her parents hadn't known these things about each other.

"Actually, I like having you here, Pia," Willow admitted. "At least my parents had to act civilized. But things have gotten so much worse since you're gone. I don't think they're gonna make it."

"Please, girl. If anybody's got hope to make it, it's your parents. Your mom's a pastor."

"And? You act like people of the clergy don't get divorces . . . they do," Willow stated emphatically before changing the conversation. "Forget me. What's going on with you? Please tell me that creepy guy your mom liked isn't around anymore."

"No, I told my mom I wouldn't be coming back if he was. At least she was kind enough to heed my warning for a change."

"Well, that's good. See, she loves you."

"Whatever. She just has interest in someone new."

"Well, that's good too, right?"

"No, it's not, because he seems just as crazy."

Willow shouted, "He's coming on to you too?"

"No, he's just enabling all of my mom's bad habits."

"Hang in there girl," Willow told Pia, realizing that neither one of them could control their parents, but hoping that, if they held on, things would get better.

Willow's annoying younger brother, Will, burst into her room. "Mom is calling you."

"Don't you see I'm on the phone?"

Before he could shout out the she was basically being disrespectful by telling her parents to hold on, she gave her brother a stern look. Will owed her big time. He had wrecked her car, but Willow had let her parents think she had been the one driving it.

"Well, just hurry up. I don't think it's good news."

Willow squinted her eyes, told Pia she'd talk to her later, and went into the family room, where her mother was sitting on the couch and her dad was leaning against the wall with his arms folded like he was disinterested.

"What's up, y'all?" Willow said.

"Sit down, honey," her mom told her. "Your dad and I are planning to take a break."

"That's good! Y'all need to go away for a vacation," Willow uttered. "I am old enough to stay here. I'm a senior in high school. You don't have to worry about the little brat. Y'all take some time. When you going?"

"You need to tell that girl," her father said to her mother.

"Yeah, sweetie, I don't think you understand," her mother said. "Your dad and I are gonna take a real break. He's gonna move out for a little while. We're gonna be separated."

"No!" William screamed. At first Willow didn't know what to say, but then she felt she needed answers.

"What do you mean y'all are gonna be separated? Why?" she asked desperately.

"You don't need to ask why, pumpkin," her dad said as he came over to her and lifted up her chin. Willow knew the reason why. Had she kept her mouth closed and not said anything about her parents' private sex lives, none of this would be happening.

Crying she said, "But Daddy, you love Mommy."

"This doesn't have anything to do with love," he said to her. "This has to do with what's best."

"So giving up on your family is best?"

Her mother added, "We just said we're taking a break."

Frustrated, Willow huffed, "Yeah, right! When people get separated, the next thing you know they're divorced. I'm not an idiot. Mom, aren't you gonna try to fight for your marriage?"

Willow rushed over to her mother, but her mother looked away. Willow jetted out of the house. She ran to house next door to see her neighbor Dawson. Willow banged on Dawson's bedroom window. He opened up the blinds. She motioned for him to come to the back door.

"What's wrong? What's going on?" Dawson said.

"It's my parents. They're separating!" He reached his arms out to hug her, but she pushed away. "You don't understand. If my dad leaves the house, I know he's not coming back. He's stubborn. My mom's stubborn too. She wouldn't want him back even if he wanted to come back. They'll be getting a divorce for sure."

"Breaks ain't always bad. My dad left a couple years ago, and there's been a whole bunch of peace in this house since then."

"So? I'm not your family! What's good for you isn't good for me. And you had nothing to do with your parents splitting up. If my parents separate, I'll never be able to live with myself."

"What are you talking about?"

"Because it's all my fault. I'm the one who couldn't stand them getting on me, so I got on them. And maybe I should have done that privately. Or I should've kept my mouth shut. I shouldn't have aired their dirty laundry in front of both of them, because clearly, they didn't know what was going on."

"Maybe they should have."

"I know, but I just should've stayed out of it. I just should've done what I usually do: let them fuss at me, and let it go in one ear and out the other."

"How would that have made anything better?"

"I could've handled it, and my family would still be together. But they kept pushing and belittling me, and I just got tired of them, so I pushed back. And because of my insolence, I'm gonna lose my family. Dang, I'm kicking myself, Dawson. I had to be the spoiler."

CHAPTER THREE

Encourager (Olive's Beginning)

Olive stood with Charles outside of the courthouse with her hands cupped around his face. In the pit of her gut, she was just as frightened as he was, but she wanted him to see her strength. A couple weeks ago, he was arrested at the Valentine's Day dance for having a knife and attacking Tiger, the leader of Black Oil. Charles had spent two days in juvenile detention. But since the judge thought he was a danger not only to himself, but also to his environment, the Department of Family and Children Services was recommending that he be removed from the group home.

Olive said, "Everything's gonna be okay. Just don't act all defiant. Make the judge know you feel remorseful. You're gonna be back home in no time."

"And if I don't come back?" Charles uttered in a pitiful tone.

"I'm not even gonna think about that because it's not gonna happen."

Charles's social worker and his attorney came up and said it was time for him to go inside, but as he walked up the steps, he kept looking back toward Olive with puppy-dog eyes. As strong as he was, she could clearly see his fear. When he was out of her sight, she started shaking uncontrollably.

"Oh no, we not havin' any of that," Olive heard Willow's loud voice say as she put one arm under Olive's while Sanaa took Olive's other arm.

Olive was happy to see them. She hoped their other friends, Pia Alvarez and Octavia Streeter, were on their way too. She needed all her new buddies there for moral support.

"That's right. We're getting you through this day," Sanaa said.

"I can't believe y'all showed up."

"We can go if you don't want us here," Willow said.

Olive replied, "No, I want y'all here."

Sanaa smiled and said, "Pia couldn't come, but Octavia's over there talking to Shawn."

"Shawn's so angry at me," Olive said. Shawn was Olive's foster brother in the group home. Just a few weeks ago, Shawn had taken a bullet that was meant for Charles. The two boys were very close.

"What do you mean?" Sanaa asked.

Olive hung her head and explained, "Because if I wouldn't have been involved with Tiger, none of the rest of this would be happening." Olive had dated the gang leader before she fell for Charles.

"Yeah, but you didn't make Charles try to get even with him," Sanaa pointed out.

"No, but I could've dismissed his advances when he smiled my way. As hard as I tried to keep him away, I let him in."

"Yeah, but you're acting like it's your fault that Charles has fallen so hard for you," Willow said.

"You guys don't understand. You all have parents who love you. Love is something you never wanna lose. Charles will do just about anything to keep it, and that's why my relationship with Charles is about to cost him everything."

Octavia came from the top of the stairs. "Come on, you guys. It's about to start," she said.

"How she get inside already?" Willow asked as she shook her head.

About an hour later, the judge was hearing Charles's case. The bailiff said, "Please rise as the Honorable Judge Walter Reinhold enters the court."

Olive felt her stomach drop as she stood. The judge tapped his desk with the gavel and told them all they could be seated. Olive looked around the courtroom. Shawn and Octavia sat nearby, but Shawn wouldn't even look at Olive. Ms. B, the woman who ran the group home where Olive, Charles, and Shawn lived, was also in the courtroom.

Olive truly wished all of this was a dream. She did not like the snarly look Judge Reinhold gave Charles as he peered over the bench, looked over his glasses, and stared hard. Olive knew the bold glare wasn't a good thing.

With a stern face, the judge said, "Mr. Charles Moe, I cannot believe you are in my courtroom again. What did I tell you last time, son, when you were in here for petty theft?"

Charles said, "That if I ever came before you again, Judge, you would make me regret it."

"And do you think the judge is a man of his word?" Judge Reinhold asked.

Charles nodded.

"Excuse me?" the judge said.

Charles spoke up. "Yes, sir. I do think you're a man of your word."

"Good, because I am."

The attorney said, "Your Honor, if I may speak on his behalf—"

Suddenly, the attorney representing the two younger kids in the group home said, "Your Honor, if I may. While the defendant might be remorseful, he's jeopardized the lives of my clients and needs to be removed from the home."

Charles's attorney said, "But Your Honor—"

Then Judge Reinhold banged the gavel

several times. "Order in this court. I don't need anybody to talk to me. We had a deal. Mr. Moe said he was clear on it, then he violated it. He made his choice, and now it's time for me to make my ruling. Charles you are hereby to be removed from the group home, effective immediately. Alternate living arrangements will be provided for you."

Ms. B wailed out, "Why?"

Shawn jumped to his feet and shouted, "No!"

Charles was trying to hold it together and not break down. Though Olive couldn't see his face, she knew his mannerisms. He was tearing up.

"No need in crying now, son," Judge Reinhold said. Olive felt horrible. "Hopefully this will really be the game changer so that you get your life together and don't screw it up for good. Have a great day. Court dismissed."

Judge Reinhold tapped the gavel, everyone rose, and then he got up and walked out. Charles's social worker got up and consoled him. His attorney placed his hand on Charles's shoulder and apologized.

Charles looked at them both and said, "Can I have a second?"

Olive rushed up and hugged him tight. "We gotta be able to do something about this."

"No. It's done. Just go. I'm out," Charles told her.

"You don't have to leave today, do you?"

"I can't even come back to the house. My stuff's gotta be packed up and sent to me. They're about to take me somewhere new. I'll figure this whole thing out in just a second."

"Oh my gosh, Charles baby, this is just awful!" Ms. B came over and said.

Unable to bear it any longer, Olive dashed out into the hallway. Willow, Sanaa, and Octavia followed.

"Y'all, this is all my fault!" Olive exclaimed. "I just knew it was gonna turn out like this. But he can't come back to the group home—the only home he's ever really had. Oh my gosh."

"Charles is gonna be fine," Sanaa said. "I know it might not seem like it now, but he's gonna figure this out. It's not your fault."

"Yeah," Octavia said. "He was just doing what was in his heart."

"How am I gonna get through this?"

"We're gonna be here for you," Willow said.

"Yeah, you not in this alone," Sanaa told her.

"Anything you need, you just ask," Octavia replied.

And while Olive's world turned upside down and her heart broke into a million pieces, she was able to find a bit of joy because each of her new friends was an encourager.

CHAPTER FOUR

Shocker (Octavia's Beginning)

"You!" Shawn screamed as he dashed out of the courthouse and caught up to Olive. He had his finger pointed in her face. His eyes were bloodshot, and his face held such intense anger. "Look what you've done to our brother. I could . . ."

Octavia was trying to hold him back. She wasn't succeeding. She knew he was going to blow up, but she didn't think it was going to be this bad between him and Olive. She had to keep trying to get through to him.

"Just settle down," Octavia said, trying to rationalize with Shawn.

Olive yelled, "Nah, Octavia, step out of his

way! He's got something to say to me, let him say it!"

"You darn right I got something to say to you! What? You don't think any of this is your fault?" Shawn looked at Olive with hate. He paused and then said, "But you know what? Maybe that's right, because ALL of this is your fault!"

Olive didn't flinch. "You can't make me feel no worse than I already do. What? What else you wanna say, Shawn? What you wanna do to me? How am I going to live with myself, knowing Charles has gotta move out of our house? If I wasn't fooling with Tiger in the first place, none of this would have ever happened. I know! I'm the reason why Charles is leaving now. If I could move out instead of him, I would."

Shawn snarled, "But you can't, so don't go givin' me no sob stories."

"Okay, Shawn," Octavia said, trying to pull him back. "Just calm down. You see she feels bad."

"Why don't you get outta my way!" he said as he pushed Octavia really hard.

Octavia was thrown up against the wall of the courthouse building, and she was hurt. Not only physically, but emotionally. Shawn was her boo, but now he was discarding her.

"Oh heck naw! I know you ain't gon' just throw my girl against the daggone building!" Willow yelled at Shawn.

Shawn quickly rushed over to Octavia apologetically. It certainly wasn't like Octavia didn't understand that he was really stressed out. She did, but her head really hurt, and she didn't think it was right for Shawn to push her, no matter what he was going through.

Upset, Shawn voiced, "Dang, I was trying to say I'm sorry. You know I ain't mean to do that."

"You just need to take your hot head on somewhere," Willow said.

Shawn looked at Octavia and replied, "Oh, it's like that, Octavia? You gon' let your friends come in between us like this? Well, whatever."

"No!" Octavia finally said, but Shawn put up his hands and stormed out of the courthouse.

"Let him go," Willow told her, holding her back so that she couldn't follow after him.

Octavia felt trapped between a rock and a hard place. She'd never had friends before. Unlike the other girls, who had no clue who put them on the swoop list, she knew exactly who put her there, and it wasn't like she could be mad at that person. Why? Because it was herself. She'd had the ingenious idea that the way to get popular was to have people talking about her. She'd thought that even if people were talking about her in a negative way, it was a good thing—until she was actually in that situation. She had quickly realized the harsh accusations, mean words, and disturbing looks were much more than she'd bargained for. But it did put her in a new group of girls who were in similar situations. They were all ostracized at school. They now had that in common and thus formed a unique sisterhood, and now they were at her side.

Not only did Octavia gain good girlfriends, she also connected with a guy who was falling for her—Shawn. Nonetheless, she hated that he was mad at Olive. Octavia was torn between following the guy or following her friend. Living in the group home together, Olive and Shawn were supposed to be like brother and sister. And although Olive was black and Shawn was white, like Octavia, color didn't matter, except the red blood of hatred.

Willow whispered, "I'm telling you, Octavia. I know you like him, but he just pushed you up against a wall. And right now, he's mad at our girl. So he needs to calm his little self down and apologize to both of you guys. Don't run up after him. And I'm just telling you what I know. You said you were new to the whole love thing. Let me school you. Don't let a jerk know you'll take anything."

Olive ran over to Octavia and said, "I'm so sorry. Are you okay? He's mad at me. He shouldn't have pushed you."

"Well, I don't want him to hit you either," Octavia admitted.

"He better be happy he just got out of the hospital a couple of weeks ago," Willow said, "or I would have punched him in the gut for pushing you like that."

Charles came out of the courthouse with his

social worker. Olive, Sanaa, and Willow walked up to him. That gave Octavia a chance to run to try and find Shawn.

She caught up with him when she spotted him around the corner. "There you are."

"Leave me alone, Octavia. Go on with your girls."

"How can I leave you alone? We're building something special here, right?"

"You ask me that today when I'm too broken to build anything. I just found out my brother can't even live with us no more, and I can't even imagine how that feels. I see what you're thinking. He's not my blood, so why should I care, right?"

"That's not what I'm thinking at all."

"Yes it is. People don't know Charles and I have been in and out of different group homes since we were in the second grade. For ten years, he's had my back. I wasn't always so tough. When people used to pick on me, he was right there, telling them they'd have to go through him to get to me. And when we'd get home, he'd beat me up. I didn't know what was going on, but he told me it was for my own good. One day I got tired of him hitting me, and I hit him back, and he said that's what he'd been waiting on. For me to get tough. Half the times he's been in and out of juvie is because he's covering my behind."

"Really?" Octavia said, stunned at the depth of their relationship.

"He'd always say, 'They wanna believe that the white boy's good. Let me take the rap.' And even when I fought him on it, a lot of the times he was right. People thought I was lying to cover for him and only locked him up. Crazy."

"But you know Olive cares about him."

"Please. Two months ago she was screwing half of Tiger's gang. I know you said you've been a loner and you're overwhelmed by all these people that all of a sudden care about you. Well, I'ma make it easier on you before we get too serious. Let's just be through."

Shawn walked away, leaving Octavia devastated. His news was a shocker.

CHAPTER FIVE
Tougher (Pia's Beginning)

"So Charles has got to move out? Are you serious?" Pia said to Sanaa over the phone.

Sanaa answered into her cell, "Yeah, girl. It's a mess. Olive is devastated, of course. Shawn is so angry at her."

"I'll reach out to Olive and Octavia. I know Octavia's gotta be upset."

"Yep, but I just don't want her chasing behind some guy who feels like it's okay to put his hands on her."

Pia didn't know how to respond to that. She was feeling some type of way about it. Her mom broke up with Jim because he punched her in the gut, and the new guy Pablo had been forcing her to drink, even though that probably wasn't the right way to put it. Nobody could force Pia's mom. But if she was already intoxicated, wasn't it easy to get her to drink more? Pia was hoping she wouldn't be like her mother. She also hoped her mom would get stronger, but she had no clue how to make that happen.

When Pia heard her mom wailing like she was in severe physical pain, Pia said, "Sanaa, I gotta go. Thanks for calling and telling me."

"Well, you call me back if you need me," Sanaa said before they hung up.

"Mami, what's wrong?" Pia said when she found her mom with her head in the toilet and vomit coming out of her mouth.

"What's wrong!?"

"I can't do this anymore, Pia. I gotta get help. I am so depressed. I don't have a job. I'm letting all these men use and abuse me so they can give me crumbs. Don't be like me," her mother blurted out.

Pia rocked her back and forth as if she was

her mother, and her mother was her child. "It's gonna be okay."

"How can it be okay when I always want a drink? When I wake up in the morning, I want a drink. I go to bed at night, and I want a drink. For lunch, I want a drink. I'm an alcoholic, *mi hija*."

Pia hadn't known the depths to which her mom had clung to the bottle. Her mother had done such a great job at hiding it. She knew her mother was moody. Really happy one moment, then upset and frustrated the next. Also, over the last couple of weeks, Pia's mom had accused Pia of drinking a couple of bottles when her mom found them empty in the morning after she'd passed out from drinking so much. Pia now realized her mom must have been so drunk the night before that she didn't even remember chugging the whole bottle down. There was a serious problem.

"I feel like I wanna die," her mom desperately exclaimed.

When Pia's mom said that, Pia couldn't hold back the tears that dropped from her eyes. It hadn't even been two full months since Pia had considered ending her own life. She had been at the first swoop list slumber party, and she'd seen all this pain medicine in the medicine cabinet at Willow's house. She had been about to try to overdose, but thanks to her friends stopping her, she lived to see another day.

Pia wanted to pass that same message of hope on to her mom. "You're gonna be okay, Mami. You're gonna make it. I can get you help."

"How can you help me? I can't even help myself. I'm not even in my right mind half the time, and I don't know how to fix things. We're gonna get evicted. I do what I do with these guys so we won't be on the street, but I'm tired. They want you more than they want me. I didn't even believe you at first when Jim came after you. If I'm not here, you won't have me as a burden."

"Mami, please don't talk like that." Pia started singing a song her mother used to sing to her when she was little, and it calmed her mom down.

Her mother swiftly fell asleep. Pia got up from the floor and grabbed a pillow and put it under her mom's head. Then she went straight to her phone and dialed Ms. Davis, the school counselor.

"Hey, Pia," Ms. Davis answered.

"I'm sorry for calling you out of the blue."

"No problem. I know a lot's been going on. I've already talked to Olive. Don't you worry about it. Everything's going to be okay."

"No. This is personal. You were talking about getting me into a support group for people who've been raped and for girls who have felt suicidal," Pia reminded her.

"That's right."

"Well, my mom needs a support group too. We can't afford rehab. She admitted she's an alcoholic, and I need to get her somewhere fast before she changes her mind about needing help. Can you help us?"

"Yeah, there's a great shelter in Macon. Let me make some calls to see if they've got some room. If they do, I'll call you over, and we'll take your mom down there."

"Thank you, Ms. Davis."

"Thank you."

"For what?"

"For being there for her. For coming around and understanding that therapy can be great."

Pia just laughed, remembering a conversation when she gave Ms. Davis a hard time about joining any kind of support group. But now Pia realized the swoop list had been good for her. She needed to take things a step further in her own life so she could be even stronger, not just for her mom, but for herself. She needed to put the rape in perspective and figure out how she could survive the whole ordeal. The fact of the matter was that the criminals who raped her were still out there, and maybe it was her job to pursue prosecuting them before they did the same thing to someone else. But she also needed to help her mom. She remembered a time when she was in middle school when her mom was working an honest job and supporting them. Though it might have only been one or two years, they were extremely happy. Those days didn't have to be gone forever.

A couple hours later, Pia and Ms. Davis were about to drive back to Jackson, leaving Pia's mom at the rehab center. Before they walked out the door, Pia's mom had grabbed her and said, "I love you, *mi hija*. Now I'm gonna get better for you. Don't give up on me."

Pia looked her mom in the eye and said, "Never, *nunca*."

When Pia walked out of the rehab center and got into the car, she was smiling on the inside. She'd just put her mom in a rehab center, but she didn't feel down. She felt full of hope. Her mom wanted to get better instead of letting her life continue to spiral out of control. Pia felt that was a step in the right direction. Pia was happy that they both were getting tougher.

CHAPTER SIX
User (Sanaa's Middle)

"So I finally get time to take you out, and all you gon' do is think about a girl on the swoop list?" Miles said to Sanaa with an attitude as they pulled up to the movie theater. He opened the car door to get out.

She just sat there with her arms folded, looking at him like he was crazy. "I don't wanna go to the movies anymore."

"Oh, so now you mad 'cuz I'm telling the truth?"

Rolling her eyes his way, she said, "I mean, you say 'swoop list' like it's some bad, negative, horrible thing."

"It's like you care about those daggone girls more than you care about us."

"Listen, you made me choose once, and you weren't on the winning end of that deal. Do you really wanna go there with me, Miles? Quit being jealous of my friends."

"Are you gonna get out of the car, or what?"

"I told you, I don't wanna go to the movies anymore. You killed my mood. Let's just go."

"Fine!" he said in a frustrated tone.

Deep down inside, Sanaa knew she needed to soften to Miles. He had been patient and had put up with a lot. But there was a lot going on in her world too, and she really needed him to be understanding. After seeing Octavia get pushed by Shawn, Sanaa made up her mind that in no way, shape, or form was she going to let Miles push her around.

"I'm sorry, baby," Miles said a few minutes later as they drove into an isolated parking lot near a park.

Squinting and frowning, Sanaa asked, "Where are we going?"

"We just need to talk. You say I'm not

understanding you. I want to understand. Is that cool?"

She nodded. He smiled and then parked. When he turned off the car, he leaned over to her and placed a kiss on her cheek and then on her forehead.

She squirmed in her seat a little when he planted a kiss on her lips. "We gotta stop. I'm not trying to go there with you."

"What do you mean, you not tryna go there with me? Come on, baby. It's been a minute."

"I know, but that part of our relationship is done. I don't want that anymore."

"So what? You get with your little girls and you gon' decide you gon' cut me off in that area? I mean, I'm puttin' up with a lot. I hardly get any time with you. I think they're a bad influence in the first place, and now you gon' let them get all in your mind? Come on, Sanaa. You know you want this, girl," Miles insisted as his hands roamed places that made her body respond in ways she enjoyed.

But her mind was strong, and finally she stopped the passion and screamed, "I said no!"

She opened up the car door and ran through the dimly lit park.

"You need to wait up. You don't know who else is out here."

But Sanaa didn't care. She just wanted the breeze to calm her down. Sanaa found a swing, and though she was way too big for it, she sat down and started swinging anyway, hoping that, with each lift, her problems would get lighter.

Miles called out, "How much further are you trying to push me away, Sanaa? I give you my heart. I give you my time. I'm tryna give you all of me. You don't want that. What's a brotha supposed to think?"

Sanaa ignored him and started swinging higher and higher. She was angry he was pressuring her. She needed a plan to settle him.

Finally tired of her paying him no attention, Miles yelled, "Can you get off the daggone swing?"

When she wouldn't stop, he yanked one side of the rope. The swing became unstable, and she fell off of it. With her face in the dirt, she punched the ground really hard with her fist.

Miles rushed to her side, "I'm so sorry!"

"I am too," she said in despair. "It's just not connecting. I don't know. I know you say you want to be with me, but it's on your terms, Miles. Nobody's controlling my mind but me. You talk about my friends on the swoop list like they're so horrible, but what makes me any better?"

"We used to have sex any and every which way you wanted to do it. Why you stopping?"

"'Cause those days are over. Answer me. What makes me any different from the other swoop list girls who seem to offend you so?" Sanaa questioned. Miles looked away. "Right, I'm no different. Actually if you add up all the times we were together, I probably had more than any of them, but yet you're telling me that I'm the good one? Please. I can't even look at myself in the mirror anymore. And if you can't be with me, just us having fun, in a platonic relationship, then I'm not the girl for you."

Miles looked back at Sanaa. She was eyeing him something fierce. Sanaa could read the anger all over his face, but she couldn't worry about pleasing him. In her mind, those days were over.

She stepped closer to him and said, "I'm sorry. Obviously this isn't what you wanna hear. This isn't where you want our relationship to go, but for us to be together, these are the parameters."

Miles squinted his eyes, curled up his lips in a mean way, and said, "Toni called me. I guess she wants me to get with her. As much as she wants me, she'll probably be way better than you anyway."

Sanaa slapped him across the face. "How dare you! You know what? Just take me home."

"I'm sorry, I'm sorry," Miles said after he realized calling her bluff was stupid.

"You gon' try to threaten me about Toni, who's not my friend anymore because of you? You think that's supposed to make me soften? Get with anybody you want. Toni, the sky, the dirt, whatever. I know my worth, and if you love me like you say you do, you'll go through some things. You gon' just kick me to the curb when I say one part of our relationship is over? That's not love!" Sanaa shouted, and tears started fall-ing. "Love is commitment, and you haven't gone through enough hell to have this heaven. All you wanna do is take. Quit being a user."

CHAPTER SEVEN

Madder (Willow's Middle)

An hour later, across the peaceful, rural town of Jackson, Willow was out with Dawson. They were exiting the movie theater that Sanaa and Miles were at earlier. As others came out, Willow looked around.

Not seeing the person she was looking for, Dawson asked, "What's wrong?"

She replied, "I don't know where Sanaa went. She and Miles were supposed to hang out here. I know I saw them pull up when we headed inside. She's not answering my texts. I hope she's alright."

"My company is boring you, huh?" Dawson

said to her in a teasing way. "Don't worry about Sanaa. As long as she hasn't called you, I'm sure she's alright. It's time for you and me to have fun."

"I'm not worried," Willow said as she stroked Dawson's cheek. "And you're right. It's our time. I got big plans for us."

"Well, I'm taking you out on a date. I got some plans too. Slow your roll. Let's go eat."

"Eat? That's just what I had in mind. I want you to devour me. And I can take a nice healthy bite into your neck, but that's about all the eating I wanna do. The kind of food that has something to do with you and me. You know what I'm saying?" Willow said seductively.

"You wanna add a little chocolate, whipped cream, strawberries, or somethin' somethin' to the mix?" He grabbed her hand and spun her around.

"Oh yes, I'm definitely down with that. You get me, Dawson." Willow went to kiss him.

Dawson gently pushed her away. "No. I was messing with you. We don't need to do all that. We can have fun without it."

"What? You don't like me being forceful? I'm a dream to most guys. I don't wanna pretend anymore. You like me. You've given me more attention than I have ever gotten from a guy. I wanna show you how much I appreciate it," Willow said. She stepped a little closer to him, put her hands on the back pockets of his jeans, and squeezed really tight. "I'ma be honest with you, Dawson. There's lot going on with my family right now. You know that. My dad ain't been there. I haven't even heard from him, unless you consider a wimpy little one-letter text he sent me back as communication. I was like, 'I miss you, dad. Hope you're okay. I want you to come back home soon,' and he sent back 'K'. Not 'O-K-A-Y,' no 'O-K,' just 'K.'"

"You never sent your parents the one-word text? Come on," Dawson said as he tickled her.

"Stop. I ain't tryna laugh. Yeah, I sent 'K' before, but I'm a teenager. Now I can honestly see why they don't like it. Anyway, my mom always has her nose in her Bible."

"Isn't she a pastor and all?" Dawson asked, being sarcastic.

"Ha, ha, ha. Yes, she's supposed to study the Word to get ready for her messages, and yes, she should believe and read for strength. I get all that, but she also is a mom who needs to raise kids going through a crisis because their parents are separated. When I need her, the only thing she can do is pray. It ain't changing nothing. I'm just sayin', if I could be with you. . . ," she said as she moved even closer to him.

People were walking to their cars and staring at them like they needed a room. Dawson felt uncomfortable. Willow turned his head back to hers and stuck her tongue in his mouth to irritate the onlookers more.

Willow said, "Forget them! I need you to take me away, and I think you wanna go to the place I want to take you."

Willow tried to kiss his ear, but Dawson jerked back, extremely irritated. "What the heck is wrong with you?"

"What is wrong with you? I know you're a virgin. No sweat, though. I can be a great teacher."

"It's not that!" he said as he pushed her hands from the front of his jeans.

"Well, what is it? Are you gay? I mean, if you are, that's fine, but don't be tryna get with me like you want me, giving me mixed signals and all. What the heck is it?"

"No, I'm not gay, and you ain't gotta try to figure it out. I'm keeping nothing from you. It's like I said. We can have a lot of fun without going all the way. Aren't you still reeling from this whole swoop list thing?"

"Yeah. I was with a bunch of jerks who never even meant anything to me. Me and you . . . we got something different, and I want us to increase that passion."

"I thought you said you were slowing your roll? You and your girls talked about it, and you were backing off of that."

"Yeah, I mean, it was all good for a minute. But it ain't cool when I'm alone in my bed, dreaming about you, and I'm squirming. I don't have to dream anymore. You're here with me. And trust me, if you give me a chance, you won't be fighting it. If you've got the feelings for me that I think you have, it's gonna be magical."

"Well, it is not just going to be your way. I

want to be in a two-way relationship. I'm not trying to control you. I don't want you to try to control me, and I'm not ready for all that."

"You sound like a wimpy girl."

"And you sound like a spoiled brat. If you think being with a real man, or a good man, or this kind of man is only somebody who's gonna have his way with you, think again. The jerks you been with ain't showing you a gentleman. And honestly, I'm getting real sick and tired of you selling yourself short. I ain't no punk, but I ain't tryna pimp you out, either. It's good that you want me, but don't just want my body. Baby, want my mind," Dawson told her with boldness. And that realness made Willow cringe.

"Whatever. Just take me home," she uttered as she got into his car and slammed the door, showing that she was even madder.

CHAPTER EIGHT

Stalker (Olive's Middle)

The last week had been a pretty rough one for Olive. Shawn hadn't said a word to her in the house. Even though everyone else tried to talk to her—Ms. B, the little kids who lived there, and her social worker—she didn't want to talk to anyone there.

What joy she did have came from her swoop list sisters. They texted her, even when she didn't text back. Their messages made her smile. They walked with her in the hallway, even though she didn't respond. They didn't leave her side. She appreciated that. She had thought Octavia would keep her distance. Olive had heard that Shawn ended their relationship because of Octavia's friendship with her. And although Olive knew Shawn meant a lot to Octavia, she was thankful Octavia didn't put her completely down. Inwardly, Olive just hated that she had nothing to give in return to these girls who cared. The first spark she'd had in a long time came when she saw Charles sitting in the school office.

"Hey!" she said to him in a real loud tone as she opened up the office door.

The secretary immediately told her to keep quiet. Olive motioned for Charles to come out into the hallway. She could tell by his demeanor he didn't want to, but he did. She threw her arms around him. He didn't hug her back. If her heart had any more pieces to be broken, they broke at that moment. His distance was shattering.

"I miss you. You haven't been in school. Where've you been staying?" she asked with deep and transparent concern.

"I don't want you to worry about me. I always knew you were too good for me, anyway. I wanted to try to finish my education so I could make something of myself and give you the world. But now I need you to go on and graduate and forget about me."

In a solemn tone, Olive said, "But how can I go on, knowing that you're suffering and it's my fault?"

"It's not your fault. If Tiger wouldn't have touched you, and you and I were connected before that, I still probably would've done something illegal to be able to provide a date for you. You've been in my heart for a while. But that's over, and I need you to go on."

"Why are you in the office? What do you need? How can I help you?" she questioned, trying to reach for his hand.

Charles stepped back and blurted out, "I'm withdrawing, Olive."

She froze like a block of ice. Trying to thaw herself out, hoping she didn't hear what she thought she heard, she squinted and asked him, "What did you say?"

"I'm quitting school. I gotta get a job now."

Almost pleading, she said, "No, you can't."

Charles turned away. "I need to pay my own way."

Olive walked around to face him again. "I'm sure they found some alternative housing for you."

"If you wanna call it that. One thing that desiring to take care of you showed me is that I also must have a desire to take care of myself. And I might not be able to do both, but I can do one of them. If giving up a degree right now is what I gotta do because of some bad choices I made, fine. I'll be okay. And so will you, if you just forget about me."

"But there's gotta be another way. We just got a couple months left of school."

"I don't have time to play around. If I work for a year, maybe I'll be able to get my GED and then go on to a two-year school and eventually go where I wanna go in this state. My dreams aren't over. Just right now, they're put on hold. Hear me, girl . . . I need you to forget me. Make me proud, and finish for both of us."

She could tell in his tone that he was struggling. He fully believed everything he said, but at the same time, there was still a level of care and concern he had for her.

"I can't just forget about you," she said.

He cupped her face and forced himself to say, "You're gonna have to. I'm done with you."

When Charles walked back into the office, Olive's yellow face was red. She knew she had to find the strength to be okay. She couldn't keep worrying about Charles. She couldn't ditch class and stay there to follow him once he left the building. Now she knew deep inside that she had to do something to help him. But, for right now, she had to keep going on.

As soon as she walked around the corner, Tiger stepped into view and startled her.

"You know, you need to heed his words," Tiger said. "He's doing the right thing. Leave him alone. Come back to me. Don't look like you've had any new clothes in a while."

"Yeah, you bought me nice things, but he didn't have to buy my love."

"Don't piss me off, Olive. I'm tryna give you a hand. You better take it, baby. I can make all his problems go away. If you come back to me, I will. You need to close your curtains at night, too. And quit taking them long baths. Don't let so much of your cleavage show in gym. I hate other guys staring at my girl. Smile, I watch you everywhere."

A chill of fear ran down Olive's spine. Olive looked at him like, *Are you always watching me?*

Tiger looked dead back at her and said, "What? Don't get it twisted. I know everything about you. Come back to me, so I can quit being a stalker."

CHAPTER NINE
Forever (Octavia's Middle)

Octavia was heading to the ladies' room. She hadn't been able to pay attention in class. It was hard to stay awake when she wasn't sleeping at night, so she thought she'd walk around, use the restroom, splash some water on her face, and be revived.

When she saw Olive jerking away from Tiger and rushing down the hall with urgency, she jetted to meet her. "You okay?"

Hysterical, Olive blurted out, "No. He's never gonna let me go. I know he put me on that list, Octavia. I did what he told me to, and then he sold me out. I just know it. I'm not able to prove it, but I know it, and he thinks I'm gonna go back to him . . . Never!"

"You don't have to. It's over."

"It's so easy for you to say," Olive said. "The fool just threatened me. If I don't get back with him, he's made it clear he'll force me. I don't know what to do."

"There's gotta be another way," Octavia said, throwing her arms around her upset friend. "You don't have to give in to a jerk. If he put you on that list, he doesn't deserve you back . . . ever."

"I know that's right," Olive said as she lightly bumped Octavia in the arm. "Who do you think put you on the list? Have you figured it out yet? I can't just let you stand up for me. All of us need to figure out who put us on there, and we need to let them know that they can't get away with it!"

At that moment, Octavia felt so uneasy. She didn't want to tell who put her on the list. She knew one hundred percent who did, but if she let it slip in any way that she was the culprit, she knew the girls she'd grown to love would leave her.

Avoiding the drama, Octavia said, "Ooh, look at the time. I better get on to the restroom and get to class. Let's talk later."

"Oh, okay," Olive said, surprised that Octavia started rushing all of a sudden.

Octavia went to the sink in the restroom and splashed water all across her face.

"Why was I such an idiot and placed myself on the darn swoop list?" she said to herself in the mirror. "And why didn't I come clean with them a long time ago? Now I can't ever tell them. They're gonna think I'm phony. If I could just talk to Shawn . . . I gotta go talk to Ms. Davis. Yup. She's gotta help me figure this out."

After Octavia dried off her hands, she left the restroom and went to Ms. Davis's door. She could see Ms. Davis was in there with another student, but waved. She was so happy when Ms. Davis smiled and put up one finger like, *Just give me a second. I'll be right with you.* That's all Octavia needed. She knew Ms. Davis would help her figure this thing out. She couldn't sit down and wait. She paced back and forth, wondering how she would even reveal to a lady she held in such high regard what a fraud she was.

About five minutes later, the other student walked out. Ms. Davis motioned for Octavia to come on in. "How've you been?"

"Not great."

"Well, talk to me about it. Sit down."

Pacing, Octavia uttered, "I can't sit. I'm stressed. I'm losing everything."

"What do you mean?"

"This whole swoop list thing. I mean, I almost came right out and said it, but I didn't actually say it. I think you know that me being on the swoop list . . ."

"Get it out. Talk to me. And I don't know any more than what you want me to know. Don't make any assumptions."

"Well, Olive asked me who put me on the swoop list. I think they're all tryna find out who messed them over. You know, at first we were angry about being on there—well, everybody but me. And then you might say, well, 'why are you not angry about being on there?' My answer is a mess, Ms. Davis."

"Okay, you're not really making any sense. Slow down, and tell me what's going on."

"I put myself on the list, okay?" Octavia shouted out and popped herself in the head in shame. "I thought it was gonna make me popular. I thought it'd change my status for good in this school, and I know I'm about to graduate and I shouldn't care, but I did. I didn't wanna end up these last months in high school as a dork. So, I embellished. Told some lies about myself to get on the list, and while it was more than what I bargained for at first, because I didn't like the negative attention, it's given me four girls who are my BFFs. And for someone who lives with her dad, good girlfriends mean the world. I think we could be close for life, but they won't desire to associate with me at all if they find out what I've really done."

"You want relationships based on honesty, correct?"

"Yes."

"And you trust the friendships that you guys are building?"

"Yes."

"Well, what you've done is bothering you. And while you now realize that you probably made the wrong choice in putting yourself on this list, you had some valid reasons at the time for why you felt that was the best way to go."

"So you think I was right to put myself on the list?"

"No. I'm not saying that at all. But I'm saying now that it's done, and you've got relationships that you care about, focus on keeping them, not on what you cannot change. Your friends are hurting because someone put them on the list, and they think you're in the same boat. Share the truth. They'll probably understand more than you think."

Shaking her head, Octavia said, "What if they don't understand? What if they kick me out of the group? You know, Olive didn't even want me in it in the first place. I don't know. I really love these girls so much. I was excited about this relationship with Shawn. You know, one of the guys who lives in the foster home with Olive, but he's not even talking to me right now. As bad as that bothers me, it would kill me if I lost the swoop girls forever."

CHAPTER TEN

Stronger (Pia's Middle)

Pia was cleaning up their two-bedroom apartment with glee. You would have thought a queen was coming. She was so excited. Today was the day her mother was coming back home from rehab. It had been two weeks. Had her mom been sober when she left, she probably would have demanded that Pia go and stay somewhere other than in their home alone. But because she was not in her right mind, Pia's mother never asked her where she was staying while she was in rehab, and since it wasn't brought up, Pia stayed alone.

During the whole time, she wasn't actually

by herself every minute. Stephen, a boy from school that Pia had her eye on, checked in on her, took her to get groceries twice, and kept her company. He was a gentleman. No pressure. No expectations. Just a good friend. As Pia anxiously waited for her mom to return, she reflected on her time with Stephen. Not only was he a hunk, but he was also caring. She secretly hoped to see him soon.

Her mind drifted from Stephen when one of her mother's girlfriends, Maria, honked the horn outside the apartment. Pia looked out of the window and saw her mother waving good-bye to Maria. Pia opened the door, and her mother rushed to her and hugged her so tight.

Her mom said, "Oh my baby! I missed you. *Dame un beso mi hija.*"

"I missed you too," Pia explained, giving her mom a kiss on the cheek.

Her mother was so complimentary, the opposite of what she'd been for the last couple of years. Pia was also impressed that her mother looked so refreshed and rehabilitated. They sat down together at the kitchen table, and they ate the tamales and fajitas that Pia had fixed. More importantly, Pia's mother told her about her time in rehab.

Smiling at Pia, her mom held her hand and said, "I'm so glad I went. It was hard, but I feel renewed. Thank you for taking care of yourself while I was gone. As my mind started clearing up, I worried about you because I realized you were home alone. I knew you could handle you, but I had to fight to get better sooner than later to be home with my baby girl. What helped was that they gave me your messages. All I needed to see was that you were okay. That gave me comfort. Thinking of you gave me the will to stick with the rigorous program. I made it through. Still a long way to go, but—"

"But, you're better, Mom," Pia countered, desperately wanting her mom to be proud of herself.

Her mother nodded. "Yes, and they've got a program that helps me find a job. I already put in some applications. I'm going to interview tomorrow for a waitress job."

Beaming with pride, Pia replied, "You'll get

it, Mom. I know you will."

Smiling, her mom said, "But enough talking about me, Pia. I owe you an apology."

"No, you don't, Mom. That alcohol was leading you. I understand that."

"But that's still not enough. I want to make it up to you."

"You are. You went to rehab. You're talking about getting a job. You look better than you ever have. To have my mom back before I graduate from high school is the best gift in the world."

Shaking her head in despair, her mother said, "Yes, but so much has happened to you that I haven't dealt with as a mom."

Confused, Pia flinched and responded, "I don't know what you mean."

"I want to file some reports," her mom said. "If Jim came on to you—"

Getting upset, Pia interrupted defensively, "If? Mom, he *did*."

"You're right, baby," her mom said with compassion. "And we need to report that. There needs to be a restraining order so that he cannot come over here again. He hasn't been here in the last couple of weeks, and I don't want him to come over here again, ever. In addition, those guys who took your innocence, we got to file that, too."

Standing up and scared to death, Pia said, "But Mom, it's going to open up a whole can of worms. I've already been through the mud, being included on some crazy list at school. We never talked about it because it was so much other stuff going on, but I can't take what exposing the rape will do."

Pia's mom stood beside her and stroked her back to calm her down. "You can't take it by yourself. But if I'm beside you, we can make it through anything. You deserve to have your honor intact. And those boys who are still out there deserve to be punished."

With her eyes watering up, Pia said, "Do I have to, Mom?"

Mirroring her daughter's disdain, her mom said, "Don't you want to?"

"If you think I should, then I will," Pia said as she exhaled.

"That's my girl," her mother said to her.

As they sat back down and ate in silence, smiling at each other, Pia was proud of her mom. She was talking about dreams, hopes, and goals. She was asking Pia about graduation and prom. She was being a mom. She wanted to avenge the wrong done to her daughter. Pia felt good. If her mother could turn things around, she could find a way to not be scared to file claims against the ones who had wronged her. Now that her mother was better, she could face anything and be stronger.

CHAPTER ELEVEN

Destroyer (Sanaa's Ending)

As Sanaa sat in a counseling session with Ms. Davis and the four other swoop girls, she felt the weight of the world on her shoulders. As the subject "do unto others as you would have them do unto you" came up, Sanaa reflected on her friendship with Toni. Sanaa had always considered herself a great friend, but she knew she'd really let Toni down. As much as she wanted to detest Toni for the altercation the two of them got in a few weeks ago, she knew it was at least partially her fault.

"What are you thinking, Sanaa?" Ms. Davis asked.

"Yeah, girl, you're mighty quiet," Willow stated with a little funk in her attitude.

Nonchalantly, Sanaa uttered, "I don't really have much to say. I'm cool listening to everybody else."

"Ah, you got something to share," Willow said, rolling her eyes Sanaa's way. "We all being real. Don't kill the party. I'm telling y'all about my parents' separation. Olive is talking about how it feels to feel abandoned. Octavia is talking about how back when she was in middle school she used to cut herself because she felt so alone. Pia mentioned her mom just got out of rehab. And you won't say nothing? We supposed to believe yo' crap don't stink? All can't be right in your world."

"Ease up off of her," Pia said, lightly tapping Willow's arm.

Ms. Davis forcefully said, "That's right, Willow, be respectful. If she doesn't want to share, she doesn't have to share."

Teasing but serious, Willow laughed and said, "Bull. Come on, Ms. Davis. I'm just sayin'. Either we all going to share and be transparent, or we all need to keep our business to ourselves."

"Okay, okay," Sanaa said, frustrated with the pressure. "If you must know, I ain't saying nothing because I didn't want to hear what y'all have to say about it."

"No one here is going to condemn you," Ms. Davis said with a reassuring tone.

"I know," Sanaa replied with a smile, "but I guess I felt guilty."

Everyone was looking at her to elaborate. And even though she still didn't want to, she knew it might help. So she held her head down, took a deep breath, and looked straight at them.

"Spit it out, Sanaa!" Willow shouted.

"Why you always so brash with everybody?" Sanaa quickly snapped back.

"Because we're about to graduate, and this has been a crazy year. If we going to have any kind of friendship, we need to keep it real, right?"

"Yeah, Willow, but it's not what you say, it's how you say it," Sanaa told her.

Willow bluntly scoffed back, "So you some baby now? You want me to spoon-feed you the thoughts going through my mind? All of us are sharing and trusting each other with what we say. Why should I be alright with you keeping everything all bottled up?"

Sanaa let the tears well up in her eyes. She said, "Fine! You wanna know my thoughts. I feel like a traitor."

"Yeah, we know you feel bad that you didn't tell Toni that Miles liked you instead of her," Olive said, wondering why that was difficult for Sanaa to share.

Sanaa breathed hard. "No, dang it, this isn't about Miles. I feel guilty because the close friendship that we are forging, I never had this close a bond with Toni. Bottom line, I've let you guys in in a whole lot of ways that I never have with her. And I used to call her my best friend."

"Well, she's just a jealous wench anyway," Willow said.

"Willow," Ms. Davis added. "Be nice."

Willow mouthed "sorry" to Ms. Davis and said, "I just want her to ease up on herself. It's hard to give your heart to somebody you know doesn't have your back."

"Right, right, right," Sanaa said. "But

maybe, if I'm honest with myself, it wasn't just about her being jealous of me. Maybe I was jealous of her too. I think the competition went both ways. We both were competing with each other. I wasn't trying to hurt her when it came to spending time with Miles, but—" Sanaa became extra emotional.

"It's okay," Ms. Davis said when Sanaa couldn't finish her sentence.

Whimpering, Sanaa said, "I just want to be a better person, ya know? And I care about each of you guys. I give all of you my all, and it's not about a competition. I know how blessed I am to have you all. Though I truly detest that we got here from being on that crazy list, I know I wouldn't trade it for anything. And I don't know if I can salvage anything with Toni because I blamed her for so long for everything. I now see that so much of it was my fault too."

"Girls, if you don't want to repeat bad patterns in your life," Ms. Davis began, "sometimes it's good to look out the back door of your life, sit there for a minute, and think about your past mistakes. Not to make yourself feel bad, but to figure out how to be better than your bad choices."

They all nodded. Sanaa really took in Ms. Davis's wise counsel. What was done was done, but her past didn't have to break her.

As soon as they finished their session, Willow asked Sanaa if they could hang out. The last period of the day was about to end. Sanaa was shocked that Willow was so warm and fuzzy. Willow had moved on. Sanaa loved that they could vent with each other and not hold grudges.

"Sure," Sanaa said. "I just need to take care of something. I'll meet you at my car, and we can grab something to eat and chat."

"I didn't mean to come off so mean," Willow said. "That's just me, ya know, a little brash. I'm working on it."

"I got you."

Sanaa went to Toni's classroom. When the last bell rang and Toni came out, Sanaa tried to call her over. Toni walked the other way as soon as she spotted her, so Sanaa jogged up behind her.

"I just wanted to apologize."

"What? For scratching up the back of my neck?" Toni yelled as she pulled her hair up to show Sanaa her marked-up neck.

Sanaa frowned. "No. For not being a best friend."

Toni stuck her finger in Sanaa's face and shouted, "Well, how about this, I don't want your stinky apology! Shame on me for allowing you into my world. You let me down, but I'm not going to let you do it again. I don't want or need your pitiful friendship. Stay the heck away! You are a taker and a loser and a destroyer!"

CHAPTER TWELVE

Bigger (Willow's Ending)

Willow watched with a broken heart as Sanaa's ex-best friend just told her off. Willow had so much going on in her own life: problems with Dawson, the embarrassment of leaving the dance team after the swoop list came out, and now the sadness of her parents' separation. In spite of all that, she still had a big heart for what was going on with her friend.

Willow cared deeply for Sanaa, so much that she went over to her and said, "I'm so sorry, girl."

Sanaa tried to hide the hurt, but then she fell into Willow's arms and cried. "It's all my fault she doesn't want to be my friend anymore.

But thank you. You and I just fussed, but yet here you are, being there for me. I don't even deserve your friendship."

Sanaa cried harder. Willow patted her back. She wanted to remove Sanaa's pain. Willow was shocked that she felt that type of connection.

Willow tried to encourage. "None of us really deserve anything. I guess when I look back at my own mistakes, that's one thing I know. We all fall short. The stuff my mom preaches is in me. We just all need to do better so we don't fall as short continually. I wish I had a friend like you."

"Well, you got me now," Sanaa said as she turned around and started walking out of the school. Willow followed after her.

"I know, and I want to make the most of it. We got two more months, and we're going to graduate. You and Toni are history. Don't stress over her. She's so full of drama. Be glad," Willow boldly stated.

"But how can I? I'm not perfect. I've been closer to you guys in a couple months than she and I ever were over years. And that so bugs me," Sanaa admitted.

Willow nodded. "I know it bothers you, and I get you're hoping you fix things with that she-devil."

Sanaa ignored Willow's little joke. "I do want to fix it, Willow. But how can I? You saw what she just told me."

"If she means that much to you, keep praying. I understand that you have to have hope for what is important to you. I'm holding out hope for my parents. It's their anniversary today. My dad is coming over for dinner tonight, and my mom texted me. I know she misses him."

"Wow. I hope it works out," Sanaa said with sincerity.

Willow could sense the genuine care Sanaa had for her family when she squeezed her hand. The two of them went to IHOP to get some afternoon pancakes, and Willow asked, "How's Miles?"

Sanaa said, "Worse than you and Dawson. I know that much."

"Oh please, girl," Willow replied. "There is no me and Dawson."

"Uh, there is no me and Miles."

"Well, that makes sense because last week we were wondering what happened to you guys. You were supposed to be at the movies."

"That night the bottom came out of our relationship."

"Yours too? That's when me and Dawson broke up," Willow said.

The two girls shared. Sanaa explained how Miles wanted to take their relationship so far again and again, and she was not having any more of that, but he couldn't understand. And in contrast, Willow admitted that is exactly what she wanted with Dawson, but Dawson wanted to put on the brakes. The two girls laughed.

"We need to trade boyfriends," Willow joked. "Then we'd both be satisfied."

"Well, help me see your side." Sanaa asked. "With everything we went through with the swoop list, we talked about putting on the brakes. You got a boyfriend who's patient and not wanting to push you. Why is that a problem?"

"Psh, girl, I could ask you the same thing. Why is it such a big deal that Miles wants to keep making you feel good? You started him down that path, and you just want to cut him off completely and expect him to understand? Why is that okay?"

"I don't know if there is any common ground. It seems like either you are having sex or you're not having sex," Sanaa uttered. "How are we going to get past this? It's not like you don't like Dawson. It's not like I don't like Miles, but the way we're looking at the relationships is just oil and vinegar, no mix at all."

Willow held her head down, thankful that the waitress came over and gave them their food. It took her a second to really realize that Sanaa had a good point. She had been through a lot. Dawson was being patient. Why did it have to be her way or no way? At the same time, Sanaa took a bite, and it dawned on her that Willow had a point. She needed to continue talking to Miles and at least hear him out, even if she knew she wasn't going to change her mind right now.

"Guess we got a lot to think about," Sanaa said as she dropped Willow off back at home.

"Yeah. But I hear you. Taking things slow isn't a bad thing," Willow uttered.

"And I hear you. I'm being understanding, even while I'm looking out for myself. Everybody who doesn't think like me is important too."

"I'm glad we can share honestly with each other."

"Yeah," Sanaa said.

When Willow went inside, her heart was racing. She had seen her dad's car, but she didn't know what she could say to get her parents back together. But she didn't have to say anything. When she walked into the living room, she found her mother and father locked in a kiss. Somehow they were working through it, and she knew then that that's what she wanted to do in her own life: work through the drama, continue to grow, and not be bitter from the madness in her life, but instead become better and bigger.

CHAPTER THIRTEEN

Giver (Olive's Ending)

"Thank you," Olive said to Octavia when she pulled up to the front of the courthouse.

"You don't have to thank me," Octavia replied, shocked that Olive had arranged a meeting with Judge Reinhold, the judge who required Charles to move out of the group home.

Olive didn't know what she was going to say to the judge. She just had to plead with her whole heart, and she hoped that he would hear it. She'd surprised herself by getting an appointment with him. Though, in order to get the appointment, she'd told him she was doing an interview for the school newspaper. But she didn't mind being a little dishonest because this was a big deal.

"Come on in, young lady," Judge Reinhold said with glee, so opposite of the tough man she remembered from earlier in the month. "You want to put me in the school newspaper for Jackson High? I must say I'm honored. I'm a product of JHS. Class of nineteen-eighty."

Feeling really bad now, Olive fessed up. "Sir, I have to apologize, but I'm not here for the school paper. The only way I could get an appointment with you was to say something like that. I do go to Jackson, but I am here for this guy."

Olive turned around her phone, which had a big picture of Charles. The judge's pale face started turning red. Olive braced herself to get thrown out.

Quickly, she started explaining, "I'm sorry. Please don't be mad at me, sir. I definitely didn't mean to be deceitful, but I need your help."

He grunted, "Help with what? If you're coming to lobby for this young man, you've come to the wrong place. I gave him plenty of chances."

"I know, Your Honor, but please," Olive uttered as she saw Judge Reinhold soften when she gave him respect. "Sir, if I can simply tell you a quick story. Your clerk said I have fifteen minutes for the interview. I only need ten."

He sat back and studied her. She smiled and clasped her hands together. He motioned for her to go ahead and start talking.

Olive began, "Charles and I have a weird relationship."

"You're his girlfriend, I presume?"

"I don't know. I was his foster sister. You see, I don't have parents either. And Judge, I don't know how your upbringing was, but just imagine having no parents. No one there to want you, and no one there to care. Think what that would do to you as a kid. In a group home, you sometimes see other kids getting adopted, but you get passed up time and time again. That is my life. That is Charles's life."

"And that's supposed to be an excuse for reckless criminal behavior?" Judge Reinhold asked.

"No, sir. Not at all. But hopefully it'd be an excuse for a great judge with a tremendous reputation in this county to give some more grace to a boy who only got a little hot under the collar because he was trying to help his friend out."

"Explain."

"I was with the wrong kind of guy. A guy who is known for being over a gang. Probably doing real criminal activity in our school. But he was the only one who was giving me things. It's hard when you never had new shoes or money to get your hair and nails done. You're not cool when you look like a bum. Naturally, you cling to someone who can give you those things, at whatever cost. But I was abused in tons of ways, and when the guy finally broke it off, Charles stepped in to defend my honor. I couldn't see how bad I was spiraling out of control. And then the guy wanted to retaliate, and all the things he said he was going to do to me, to Charles, to anyone who got in his way, were scary. So Charles did what was in him to do, and that's stand up and protect those he loves. If anybody deserves to be put out of that house, it's me. I brought the madness to our group home, not Charles."

Judge Reinhold breathed deeply, clearly moved, yet now faced with a dilemma. "I see."

Olive saw Judge Reinhold's demeanor soften even more. He unfolded his arms, and he sat up in his chair to listen more intently. While she hated that she had to reveal the worst things about herself, to save Charles she was willing to do it. So she kept going.

Olive continued, "Judge, I'll leave the group home, but Charles needs to be there. I know there has been a new placement for him, but it's not a good situation. He's dropped out of school. We're two months from graduating. He's got a 3.1 GPA. He can go to college on the Hope Scholarship, but he's got to graduate. Now he doesn't even want to do that. He just wants to get a job to take care of himself. Your one decision is setting his life on a course that is not what you intended at all."

"Well, I've made my ruling," Judge Reinhold shared, refolding his arms.

Olive stood up, and her eyes watered up. She clutched her hands together, not knowing what to say to the judge so he could really understand her, but she knew she had to try.

When she didn't move, Judge Reinhold said, "Well, thank you. I heard you."

"But you're not going to change your mind? You're not going to give him another chance? You're not going to reconsider this?"

"I will touch base with his case worker, and maybe I need to reevaluate."

"Thank you, Judge! Thank you!"

"I didn't say I was going to change my mind," Judge Reinhold made clear.

"Your Honor, the fact that you're going to consider it is big." Olive went around the side of his desk and hugged him tight.

He was overwhelmed and said, "Okay, I can see that if Charles has you in his corner, he is not as alone as he thinks. And I'm proud that it seems you've learned from your past choices as well. With your heart and selflessness, you've given me faith in our youth. You're not a taker. Clearly you're a giver."

CHAPTER FOURTEEN

Fixer (Octavia's Ending)

"You! What are you doing here?" Octavia said as she opened up the door to her trailer. She was stunned to see Shawn standing outside.

"Your dad invited me," Shawn said as he turned around and waved to Ms. B, who drove away.

Octavia was extremely confused. She hadn't talked to Shawn in a week. She barely talked to her father. He was so busy as an assistant manager at Wal-Mart this year that she barely saw him, and she'd never really talked about either of her parents to anyone. She wasn't embarrassed that she was raised by a single father, but she was saddened that her mother had taken off with her drug-pusher boyfriend.

Turning to her father, Octavia asked, "Dad! How'd you know about Shawn?"

"I didn't. But he called the house a couple days ago, and he and I just started talking, so I invited him over for us to get to know each other. Come on in, young man."

Not only was Octavia overwhelmed that her father had invited Shawn, but she couldn't believe he'd shown up. He'd told her they were through, and he'd put his hands on her. She hadn't chased him, so she was baffled why he had called in the first place. She wondered, what did he want? And the bigger question was, what was she willing to give him?

Octavia quickly put her doubts and questions aside as she melted, seeing his nicely tanned body stroll in and shake her father's hand. She surely knew she missed him. Now it all made sense that her father was having her clean up and set the table for three. She thought the guest would be some lady he was going to introduce her to, but he certainly had her on this one.

They sat at the table. Octavia didn't want to eat because she didn't want to get food all over her mouth and be embarrassed. Also, she didn't know what to say. She didn't want to sit there like a bump on a log, but she hated appearing nervous. Feeling uncomfortable, she played with her food, sat there, and smiled. It didn't much matter that she wasn't adding to the conversation. Her father and Shawn were having no problem finding things to talk about. But when her dad asked Shawn about his parents, a little bit of the green beans that she had managed to put in her mouth flew out. One long piece landed on her father's cheek.

As she handed her dad a napkin, she whispered, "Don't talk to him about that."

Shawn overheard her and said, "No, it's fine. Sir, I'm an orphan. I live in a local group home. I hope it's not a problem that a poor pauper is wanting to date your daughter and all."

"Why would it be? I was an orphan too."

"You were?" Shawn said as his eyes opened wide.

"I didn't have to live in a group home. My

uncle raised me with his wife, but they weren't my parents. They took off, and I guess I repeated the cycle by seeing the same traits in my own wife. She took off on me and Octavia."

Shawn said, "Wow, I didn't know that. I don't talk about my family, so I never pressed Octavia to talk about hers."

Her father shared, "I find looking back on our past can give us strength for our future. I'm not ashamed that my parents left me. I'm just thankful that my uncle was there for me. Honestly, since I had Octavia young, it would have been mighty easy for me to slip out too. But there was something inside of me that understood what it is to be like to be abandoned, and it wouldn't let me do that to anybody else. And talking to you, I think you got those same cool traits."

"So what you're saying is I don't have to be bitter?" Shawn asked, tuned in to the advice.

Her father said, "Right. Believe it or not, if you put in some effort, you're going to be a better person than your parents. Someday you'll be a better dad, and hopefully now you'll be a better boyfriend."

The way her father stared at Shawn made Octavia giddy all over. She felt her father knew Shawn needed to step it up a notch. She didn't know if Shawn had confessed something to her father or if he was just guessing, but he was dead on. Shawn was taking it in.

When Octavia's dad got up to clear the table, Shawn touched her hand and mouthed the words "I'm sorry."

Her father suggested, "It's a nice March night out there. Why don't you two go for a little stroll? Don't get too far. Octavia, show him the walking trail behind the trailer park. Y'all come on back in about an hour, and I'll get you on home, son. That sound good?"

"Yes, sir," Shawn said. "And thank you for the talk. I needed to hear that."

Her father smiled. "Above all, you two be good friends to each other."

They nodded before the two of them stepped outside for the walk. Octavia was still reeling from the exchanges between her two favorite men. She did hope her friendship with Shawn could get better.

After a few minutes of silence, Shawn said, "I've been a jerk. I know I gotta lighten up on Olive. And even though I hope you will forgive me, I definitely understand if you can't. I didn't mean to be so aggressive with you that day at the courthouse. I've kind of been kicking myself ever since. I just wish my world could be right, but it seems like it's always messed up. If I could get things back on track with you, that would be a huge step in the right direction."

"I do want us to be close. I want things to be right between us, but I'm not who you think I am. I've got some issues."

"You?" he teased.

"Yeah, me." Octavia popped him lightly as she bantered back. "The whole swoop list thing."

"I don't care about that dumb list."

"You don't understand. I'm holding a big secret over it, and when people find out, nobody is going to like me."

He stopped walking and turned to her, "What? Trust me. Tell me."

All of sudden Octavia blurted out, "I saw the posting online for the swoop list. People could e-mail who they thought was the easiest girl in the school and argue their case. I made a new e-mail address, so it couldn't trace back to me. Then e-mailed and said 'Octavia Streeter belongs on this list more than other girl in the whole state!' So, I put myself on the list, okay? There!"

"Oh that? I sort of figured that."

"You did?"

"I ain't really figured out why, but who else would have done it? You have no enemies. I know for sure you're a virgin."

She blushed and looked away. "When the girls find out, they're going to hate me."

"I can't tell you how they're going to feel, but they know your heart. You can make this right. Octavia, you're a fixer."

CHAPTER FIFTEEN
Better (Pia's Ending)

It was the last day of March, and Pia was feeling good about things. Tonight was going to be another big slumber party at Willow's house for the swoop list girls. Things were getting better for everyone. Sanaa wasn't sweating the fact that she couldn't control how other people felt about the decisions she'd made. She could only get better from them. Willow was thankful her parents were giving it another go. Olive was ecstatic that Charles was going to be home for the next couple of months to graduate. Octavia seemed excited that her father liked Shawn, and Pia was happy too. Her mother had started finding a job, and the landlord was working with them on paying back the rent owed.

Pia was running around the corner in the hallway to get to class when she heard squeals. When she saw some of the swoop girls, she started running towards them. "What's going on?"

"It's Stephen, look!"

Pia looked down and saw her friend's face bashed in, barely recognizable. She bent down by him. "Oh my gosh! What happened?"

She helped Stephen to his feet, and he said, "Some of the guys know I gave statements to the police about them raping you. They're trying to shut me up."

"Oh my gosh! You're gonna have to take back what you said. I can't let you get hurt over me."

"But you were hurt. Because I didn't stop the rape back then when I had a chance, I can't get all of that out of my mind. Today those punks jumped me from the back. One of them covered up my eyes with a dirty sock, like I can't hear their voices. A black eye and a bloody nose are not gonna make me hush up. I'm going to the office to report this right now.

All of their violence is gonna be on the record. It's got to stop."

Sanaa tapped on Pia's arm and asked, "Is he gon' be okay?"

Pia nodded as she helped him hobble to the front of the school. "I don't want you to try to be some hero and keep taking abuse for me. I can take care of them. I didn't even know the cops were going to ask you anything."

"Oh, the last week they've been asking a lot of the players a lot of stuff, and word is out I'm the only one talking. They didn't even know I witnessed the rape, but I did, and I didn't make it right for you then. But I am now, Pia."

When the principal came out to speak to Stephen, the two men went into his office. Pia had to go on to class. She couldn't get Stephen out of her mind. He was helping her, maybe because he liked her, but more because he wanted to do the right thing. He was a hero in her eyes. Her heart had been hardened for so long, but now things were looking better.

Later that evening, when they were having their third slumber party and Pia was staring into the bathroom mirror at Willow's place, she thought back over the darkness she'd experienced the last few months. She suddenly realized that she had made it through that dark period. She was wiser and actually ready for the next phase of life.

"Alright, open up in there!" Willow said, standing on the other side of the bathroom door.

"Yeah, come on out. You don't want us to have to bust the door in," Sanaa said. "It's girl time!"

When Pia opened the door, she asked, "Where's Octavia?"

"Sittin' over there all melancholy," Olive smiled and said. "Something's wrong with the redhead."

"No," Octavia announced, typing on her laptop. "I'm just really enjoying our time, and I'm doing some research, and I found out where that girl, Leah, went to school."

"Is she dead?" Olive asked, searching through her purse to find the letter.

"Yeah. Her obituary is right here," Octavia said.

The girls gathered around the computer, and they were shocked to see the beautiful African American girl smiling like she had no care in the world. Silence befell them as they looked on. Pia felt sad that this girl had actually taken her own life.

"Gosh, it says right here she was a dancer," Willow said.

"And was a star student," Sanaa pointed out.

"She's survived only by her mom," Pia said.

"Looks like she had some involvement with a local gang," Olive uttered.

"But, in the end she was a loner," Octavia said.

All of them felt like they had something in common with Leah, and for a moment, things got really quiet again and even more intense. Pia wished she could have known Leah to help save her life. She sighed, realizing that Leah had helped to save her life with the little notes.

Pia said, "How could she be sending us stuff if she's not alive? I mean, clearly, she's dead. There's an obituary."

"Maybe she's not," Willow said.

"Everything she's told us, we needed to

hear—change our lives, get some faith, examine our past—but not all of us are always listening to everything she tell us," Sanaa said, looking dead at Willow.

"Yeah, I hear you. Took me a while to get there, but making the same mistakes over and over is pointless," Willow replied.

"How you doin' with Toni, anyway?" Pia asked Sanaa.

"She's still mad. But I'm so thankful I got you guys."

"Ditto that!" Olive said. "You guys gave me the strength to channel all of my passion in the right area."

"It's not like we went with you to talk to the judge," Willow said.

Olive admitted, "You weren't actually with me, but in a way you're with me all the time."

"Yeah, I clearly get that," Pia agreed. "I was only able to help my mom and at the same time understand all she went through because you guys supported me."

"So here's a question I have," Willow said. "Since we've looked back, we all know how bad being on the swoop list has been, but would you trade it? Would you change it? If you could go back, would you make sure that you weren't on it? Sanaa?"

"No," Sanaa said, looking at all of them.

"Olive?" Willow asked.

Olive responded, "No. It got me away from Tiger."

Willow said, "Octavia?"

Octavia hesitated, but then said, "A little yes, but more no. Please don't ask me to elaborate."

Willow shrugged at Octavia's weird response, but said, "Pia?"

Pia said, "Before I answer, you tell us your answer."

Willow nodded. "Obviously no, because I keep wanting to do the same things that probably got me on the list. I never could've imagined that I'd have such friendships. So, no, because of y'all too. Now you, Pia."

Pia smiled and motioned for them to grab hands. When they were all standing there, facing each other, Pia said, "No, I would not change being a swoop list girl. This list brought me you all. And because of your friendship, I'm better. Actually, I know our tight bond has made us all better."

ACKNOWLEDGMENTS

Back that thing... every one of us can learn from our past. If want to be better in this life... evaluate what you've done and do not redo your mistakes! Here's a look back to thank those who helped me all along the way.

To my parents, Dr. Franklin and Shirley Perry, looking back I'm thankful you gave me a great foundation. That foundation helped me to build greatness. To my editor, Mari Kesselring, looking back I am thankful you pour everything into getting my work to be the best it can be. To my extended family, looking back I know your deep love spills over into my writing. To my assistants Ashely Cheathum, Alyxandra Pinkston, and Candace Johnson, looking back you all are on it. Your diligence makes my work better. To my dear friends too numerous to name, looking back I know your friendship has enabled me to write about the strength real bonds can bring. To my teens, Dustyn, Sydni, and Sheldyn, looking back I am grateful I am your mother. To my husband, Derrick, looking back, I thank you for twenty golden years. Your endearing presence has helped me soar in this career. To my readers, especially the kids in Jackson, GA, looking back I'm so thankful you gave me the idea for the series. Your honesty in our sharing session helped me bless others with this tough subject. And to my Savior, looking back I'm thrilled you ordered my steps to be a novelist. The career you've given me has given my life purpose. I aim to make You proud.

ABOUT THE AUTHOR

STEPHANIE PERRY MOORE is the author of more than sixty young adult titles, including the Sharp Sisters series, the Grovehill Giants series, the Lockwood Lions series, the Payton Skky series, the Laurel Shadrach series, the Perry Skky Jr. series, the Yasmin Peace series, the Faith Thomas Novelzine series, the Carmen Browne series, the Morgan Love series, the Alec London series, and the Beta Gamma Pi series. Mrs. Moore is a motivational speaker who enjoys encouraging young people to achieve every attainable dream. She lives in the greater Atlanta area with her husband, Derrick, and their three children. Visit her website at www.stephanieperrymoore.com.